Toes is

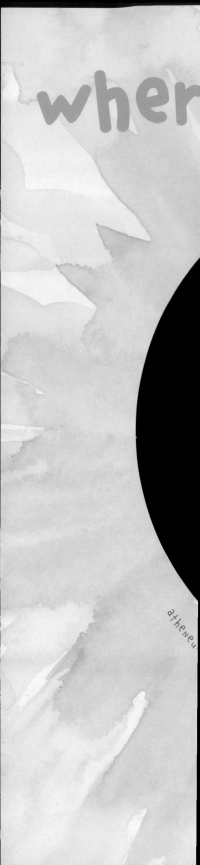

wher

atheneu

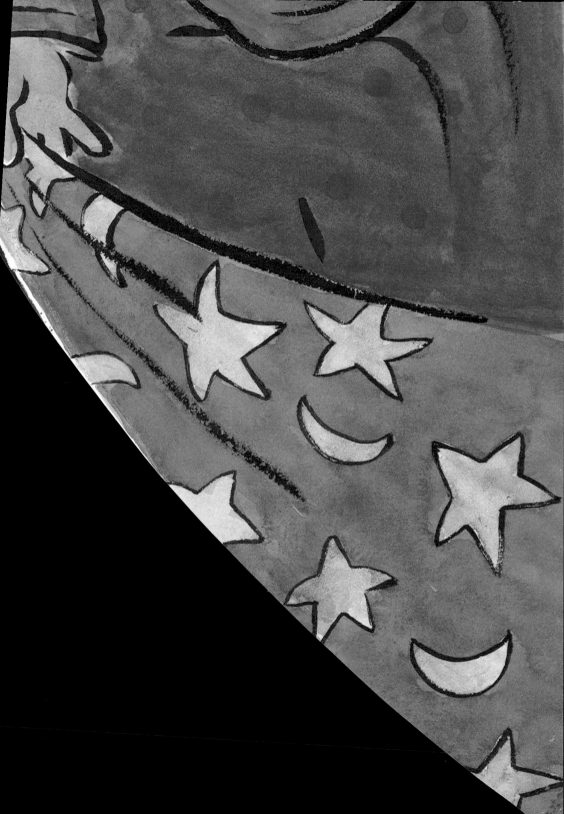

when darkness falls
and the whole world
sleeps . . .

when the sun is up and the day is his.

The mouse in his hole

knows the soft **pit pat** . . .

of Tippy Toes's step
on his welcome mat.

But nobody knows
where Tippy Toes
goes . . .

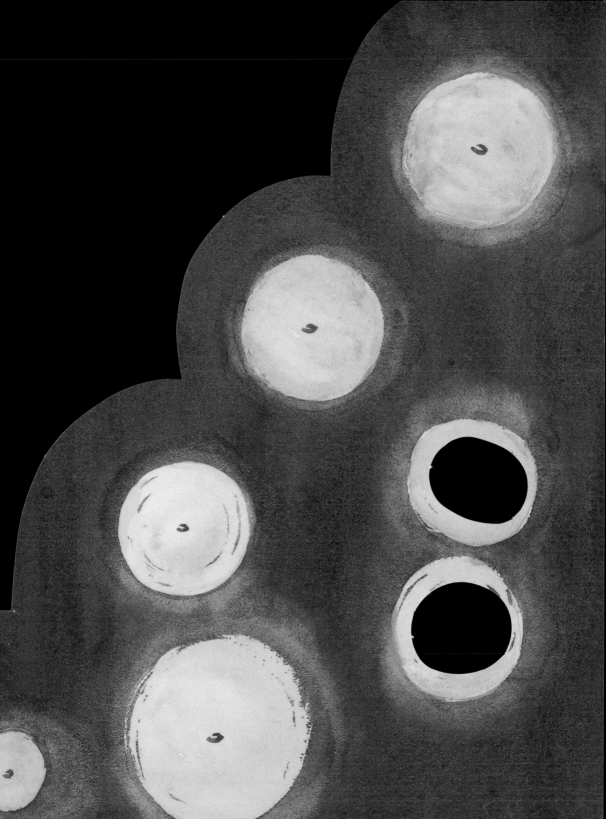

when the night is alight with firefly shows.

Everyone knows where Tippy Toes goes . . .

to escape the squirt of the garden hose.

And everyone knows
that purring snore . . .

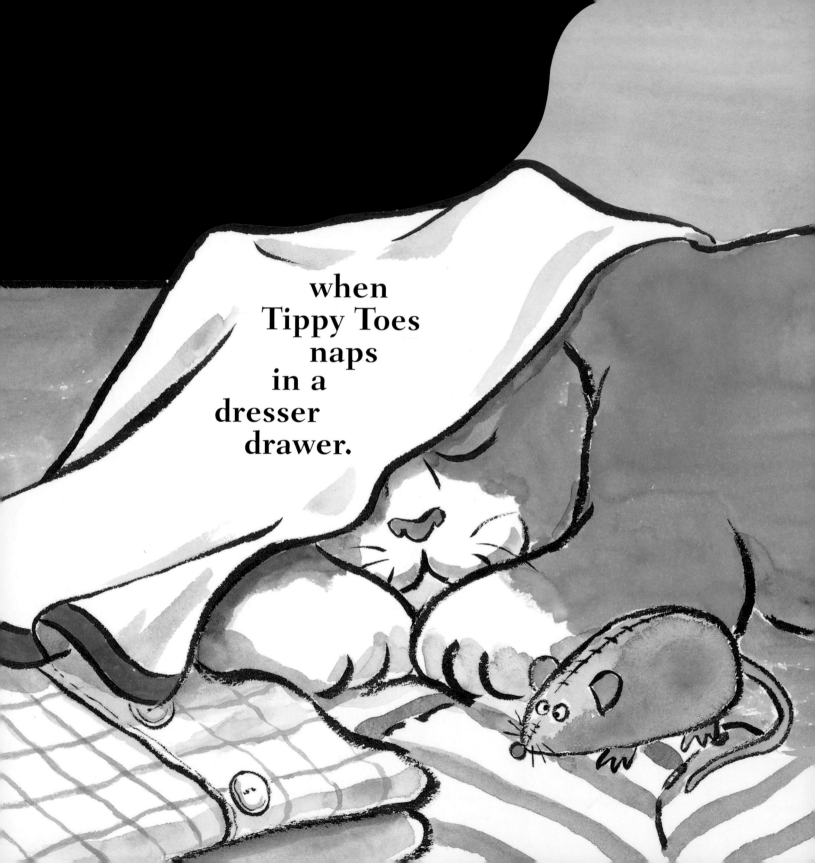

when
Tippy Toes
naps
in a
dresser
drawer.

And everyone knows

but they don't know why,

he **tippy toed** through
the blueberry pie!

But nobody knows where Tippy Toes goes . . .

when the moon
is full and
the night wind
blows.

Does Wise Owl
know,
do you suppose?

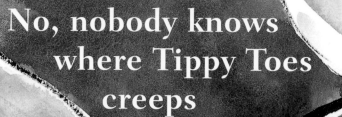

No, nobody knows
where Tippy Toes
creeps

. . . except me.

In memory of Chopper, and for Sophie

ATHENEUM BOOKS FOR YOUNG READERS
An imprint of Simon & Schuster Children's Publishing Division
1230 Avenue of the Americas, New York, New York 10020
Copyright © 2010 by Betsy Lewin
All rights reserved, including the right of reproduction
in whole or in part in any form.
ATHENEUM BOOKS FOR YOUNG READERS
is a registered trademark of Simon & Schuster, Inc.
For information about special discounts for bulk purchases,
please contact Simon & Schuster Special Sales at
1-866-506-1949 or business@simonandschuster.com.
The Simon & Schuster Speakers Bureau can bring authors to your
live event. For more information or to book an event, contact the
Simon & Schuster Speakers Bureau at 1-866-248-3049
or visit our website at www.simonspeakers.com.
Book design by Ann Bobco.
The text for this book is set in Fairfield LH.
The illustrations for this book are rendered in watercolor.
Manufactured in Malaysia
0310 TWP
First Edition
2 4 6 8 10 9 7 5 3 1
Library of Congress Cataloging-in-Publication Data
Lewin, Betsy.
Where is Tippy Toes? / [written and] illustrated by
Betsy Lewin.—1st ed.
p. cm.
Summary: Although everyone can see how Tippy Toes, a mischievous
cat, spends his days, only one knows where he goes after dark.
ISBN 978-1-4169-3808-8 (hardcover)
[1. Stories in rhyme. 2. Cats—Fiction.] I. Title.
PZ8.3.L583Whe 2010
[E]—dc22 2009024455